The Fall of Diablo
Liza Kline

First edition. October 2024.

Copyright © 2024 Liza Kline.

Written by Liza Kline.

Also by Liza Kline

A Joyous Romance
Betrothed to the Vampire King
Married to the Vampire King
Mated to the Vampire King
A Joyous Romance Series Bundle (Books 1-3)

Standalone
Cuffed - A Novella
The Trouble with Wedding Dates
The Fall of Diablo
Fated
The Princess & the Monk

Chapter 1

IT HAD BEEN THE DAY from hell. It started with Fluffy, my next door neighbor's Yorkshire Terrier, peeing on my newspaper just as I opened the front door to grab it, and ended with Evelyn Adams, a girl barely old enough to drink, becoming my boss. When Jared, my boss of almost fifteen years, had retired last week, I had expected to become his replacement. He had mentored and trained me for the last two years to do so, and had even written a glowing letter of recommendation for me that he had given to the CEO. So when I was sent a meeting request just before noon for the end of the day, I was expecting it to be good news. Instead, I had been politely asked to show Evelyn, the owner's niece and my new boss, the ropes.

I still don't know how I resisted telling everyone to take a long walk off a cliff when all I could see was red. I had nothing against the petite brunette, other than the fact that she had stolen my job. When I left the building, I had to refrain from slamming my fist into the brick wall of the parking garage...repeatedly. I needed to blow off some steam before I exploded.

I pulled my phone from my purse as I lowered my long frame into my Honda Civic and sent a quick text to my friend Rusty. 6:30? Then again, could a guy you only used for sex be considered a friend? We had been neighbors growing up until his mom had divorced his father and moved away, taking Rusty with her in the middle of ninth grade. He had moved back to the small town of Ivory, Pennsylvania eight months ago, no longer the scrawny, scraggly-haired boy of my youth. In his place was a heavily muscled man with a shaved head and a body covered in tattoos. He'd traded his ten speed in for a motorcycle and answered to the name of Diablo, which I refused to call him.

We had gotten reacquainted five months ago while I was drowning my sorrows in a bottle of tequila at the only bar in town, appropriately named The Hole. My latest boyfriend had just left me for a girl he had met in the grocery store, how clichéd was that? Who also happened to be a size two compared to my size eighteen, on a good day. Although, he swore that my size wasn't the reason he was leaving me. He was in love. More like lust. The rundown bar was the perfect place to wallow in peace. Most of the town's inhabitants preferred to drive the twenty minutes to the next town over for more modern watering holes. Places that had DJ's and theme nights.

I was close to being cut off when Rusty and a few members of the biker gang he belonged to, No Mercy, showed up. They had a reputation for partying too hard, starting fights, and

2

taking home a different woman every night. I wanted no parts of anything they were involved in. I knew I should have left before they started getting rowdy, but I hadn't been ready to start my walk home yet. Instead of getting the attention of the bartender and settling my tab, I grabbed the bottle in front of me and poured another shot.

A rough hand wrapped around my wrist as I raised the glass to my lips, making me sputter angrily. Who dared to cut me off? Rusty stood next to me, leaning arrogantly against the bar, like he owned the place. I knew that he had returned, but it was the first time I had actually seen him since high school. His eyes were still a warm chocolate brown, and there was a scar running through his left eyebrow, courtesy of a beer bottle thrown by his father in a drunken rage one night. The tattoos covering his exposed skin were intimidating but kinda sexy at the same time. He just quirked an eyebrow at me as he took the tequila from my hand.

"We can't have fun together if you're passed out." I snorted at his outrageous comment and reached for my drink.

"You don't even know who I am."

"I can't get to know you if you're too drunk to remember your own name, darling." He drawled, keeping my shot just out of reach.

"I'll make you a deal. I'll tell you what your name is, and you give my shot back." When he started to shake his head, I continued. "If I'm wrong, you can have my drink, and I'll tell you my name."

3

"What the hell? Go ahead, sweetheart. And just so we're clear, it only counts if you can tell me the name my mother gave me." I laughed at his attempt to take control of the situation. More often than not, his mother had used his full name when calling for him. Even as a boy, Rusty couldn't stay out of trouble for more than a few minutes.

"You can drop the pet names Russell William Peters; they won't work on me." I let out a drunken giggle; it wasn't every day I got to call a man by his full name. "Jesus, Rusty, I'm not that desperate that I'm going to go home with a guy who throws a few cute names my way. Especially one that used to chase me with worms. Now hand over my drink."

"Autumn?"

"That's me." I said in the sing-song voice I only used when I was drunk.

"Damn, girl." He slid the glass across the bar to me. "It's been years, and it's Diablo now. No one calls me Rusty anymore." I had the shot glass to my lips when he called himself Diablo and had to put it down because I was laughing too hard.

"No way in hell. Who the fuck calls you that?" I managed to get out between bursts of laughter. My cheeks hurt from laughing so hard.

"Everyone." His face was serious.

"Correction, everyone but me."

"Wanna bet? I'll have you screaming it by the end of the night."

"What do I get when that doesn't happen?" The tequila had me feeling a little reckless. What the hell? Why not have a little fun before my sense of respectability kicked back in?

Rusty leaned in close, his warm breath feathering against my cheek when he spoke. "Another orgasm." Who was I to argue with the promise of multiple orgasms? I tossed back my shot.

"Lead the way."

What was only supposed to be a one night stand had turned into an ongoing thing. I had won my multiple orgasms. Rusty had added his number to my phone in the morning before dropping me back at my car, with instructions to use it whenever I needed a fix. I had held out for two weeks before giving in and texting him for a repeat performance. We always went to his place; it felt weird to have someone I was only sleeping with at my house, and we never did anything else together. It was just sex. No dates or long walks through the park holding hands. The majority of the time, I asked him to take me home after we were done. That was one of Rusty's rules; he had to pick me up. He didn't give an explanation why, only said that it was easier this way. I wasn't going to argue. Not when I didn't want anyone to know that I was hooking up with a member of No Mercy. Small town gossip was vicious, and my mother and aunts would be on my doorstep, ready to stage an intervention, at the first hint that I was involved with someone they deemed inappropriate.

My phone beeped as I pulled into my driveway. I'll be there. Our texts were always short and to the point. We never talked about what we were doing, but we both seemed to be

5

happy with the way things were. At some point, I'd want a relationship again, but I'd worry about what to do when that particular urge struck later. For now, I was just going to enjoy the mind-blowing sex.

Chapter 2

I ADJUSTED THE TOWEL wrapped around my hair as I stared into my closet trying to decide what to wear. I wasn't looking to impress Rusty; I was trying to figure out what would keep me warm on the back of his motorcycle in October. Even though it had been an unseasonably warm day, I knew that the temperature would start to plummet now that the sun had set. I pulled out a pair of jeans and an oversized white sweater and set them on the bed before returning to the bathroom to dry my hair.

As I turned off the blow dryer, I heard my phone beeping impatiently from my bedroom, which was unusual. My family members were usually too wrapped up in their own lives to text me on a Friday night, and I didn't really have any close friends. At least none that would try to reach me now, unless my neighbor had locked herself out of her house again. I had her spare key for such occasions. It was Rusty, what was he doing here so early? Well hell, I'd somehow managed to lose track of time, he wasn't early at all. I quickly threw on the clothes I had put on my bed earlier, sans underwear. It wasn't like I was going anywhere but the short ride to Rusty's where my clothes would just come off again.

I slipped on a pair of knockoff fur-lined boots by the front door and shoved my phone and house key into my back pocket as I walked out the door. Rusty was slouched against his bike looking entirely too enticing in well-worn jeans that clung to his legs like a second skin and an unzipped, black leather jacket. He straightened as I approached and offered me a hand, which I ignored, as I swung my leg across the back of his bike. He settled in front of me without a word, and I mentally braced myself for the loudness that came when he started the engine.

I still wasn't comfortable on the motorcycle, so I wrapped my arms around his waist as we pulled out of my driveway. As we sped down the road, I closed my eyes and tucked my face into his back. There was something freeing about my hair streaming out behind me. When Rusty's body didn't start to lean, an indication that I should do the same to make the turn onto his road, I got worried.

"What the hell?" I yelled as we passed by the street he lived on.

"Condoms." His short reply made me thump my head against his back in frustration. Why hadn't he picked those up before coming to get me? He was as good as announcing to the entire town that we were together. Even if I stayed out on his bike, someone would put two and two together, and before morning, my mother would be calling wanting to know if it was true. There

8

was no point in trying to talk about it while we were driving. The wind would just take my words with it, and this wasn't a conversation I wanted to be overheard. We glided to a stop along the side of the building, and I waited impatiently for him to turn the engine off so I could lay into him. This wasn't part of our agreement.

"You coming in?" Rusty asked as he got off the bike.

"No." I bit off angrily. "I'd prefer to avoid the gossips, not that it matters to you."

"I can just take you home." I just stared at him. Was he being serious? The damage was pretty much done at this point. Anyone could walk or drive by and see us together. "I'll be back." He said with a shrug when I didn't answer.

I watched his long strides eat up the sidewalk before disappearing into the store. I felt silly sitting on his bike alone, and I realized that even though I was out of the direct light cast by the lone bulb in the parking lot, my white sweater still made me stand out. I climbed off the back of the bike quickly and walked over to the side of the building; at least I'd blend in a little better with the concrete behind me.

I looked around the parking lot and noticed a familiar black rag top parked by the front doors. My ex-fiancé, Kendal, was in the store. Fuck. I let my eyes close as my head fell back against the wall with a hard jolt. Our split had been amicable enough; we had just wanted different things. Plus, it had been ten years ago. Long enough for us to both move on, although my mother would still bring up the fact that he was single whenever she got the chance. We hadn't spoken since the night I had given him his ring back, but we still saw one another around town; there wasn't much hiding room in a town as small as Ivory.

I opened my eyes when a rough hand grabbed my arm. What the hell was Rusty's problem tonight? First, he brings me into town, and now he's manhandling me, like I'm some biker slut. Only it wasn't Rusty. Icy blue eyes, the complete opposite of Rusty's warm brown ones, stared back at me from behind a black ski mask. He was hunched slightly forward, giving him the impression of being a shorter man, even though he was a few inches taller than me, with the build of a distance runner.

"Scream and you'll regret it." He hissed at me, tightening his grip on my arm. He raised his left hand to reveal a revolver with a glossy black finish when I started to open my mouth. The words I had been about to spew at him angrily died in my throat. This wasn't some creep out for a cheap thrill. He meant business. "We're going to take a walk, and if you behave, you can go home tonight."

In one smooth motion, with a strength I hadn't expected from someone with such a wiry build, he jerked me away from the wall and spun me around so that I was facing the door to the pharmacy. I cried out in pain as his fingers dug into my skin when I stumbled; fear making me less graceful than normal.

"Move." He ordered, shoving me forward when I didn't get going fast enough for him. He positioned himself slightly behind me as we walked, keeping his hand clamped tightly on my arm. I could feel the bruises forming under his fingers as we approached the door.

"Don't say a word and don't try to get anyone's attention. Nod if you understand." I had to strain to hear his low-pitched voice over the whoosh of the automatic doors as we walked through them. I gave my head a quick jerk to acknowledge I'd heard him as the second set of doors opened. The fluorescent lights seemed too bright as we entered the store, or maybe it was just the shock of it all. I could hear my heart pounding in my ears as I looked around the store for Rusty.

I didn't have to look hard to find him. He was standing in line at the counter at the front of the store, waiting to check out. The teenager behind the counter looked impatient as a white-haired woman, who I recognized as Mrs. Hill, the Sunday school teacher, dug through the change in her palm. Behind her was Kendal, his eyes glued to his phone, holding a red plastic shopping basket. Rusty was last in line, keeping a healthy distance from my ex. The box of condoms dangled between two fingers as he looked around the store lazily.

"Hands in the air!" My captor's yell startled Mrs. Hill so badly that the change in her hand dropped to the floor. I watched as Kendal looked up in surprise, and Rusty just crossed his arms over his chest. "Don't make me repeat myself, or she gets it." He threatened waving the gun in the air.

I watched recognition sweep across the faces in front of me, all except the tall boy behind the counter. I didn't know him either, but I'm sure if I heard his name, I could tell you which of my high school classmates he belonged to. It was just the way small towns worked. Mrs. Hill was the first to raise her arms. I could see her hands shaking, and I wondered if it was from fear or age. Kendal let his basket drop to the floor before he too raised his hands. At least my ex didn't want to see me dead. The teenager behind the counter followed suit when he realized that neither of the men in the store were going to play hero. That left Rusty. Who remained standing with his arms crossed over his chest, the condoms on the floor forgotten.

"You have thirty seconds, tough guy." He pressed the barrel of the gun to my temple, and I had to lock my legs to stay upright.

I stared at Rusty, willing him to stop the macho bullshit and do as the guy holding the gun to my head demanded, but he stared past me at the man. His jaw was clenched in fury, and I wondered why he was so angry. It wasn't like anything would happen to him if he just let the guy take the cash. Slowly, without lowering his gaze, Rusty put his hands in the air as well.

"Open the drawer, kid." He ordered pushing me toward the counter. There was a soft thunk that had him whirling us back toward Rusty. "What the fuck was that?" The box of condoms was no longer by Rusty's feet, but instead in between Kendal's. Rusty must have kicked it when he tried to move. "Did I not make it clear to you what would happen? Or do you not care about the bitch?"

"Hey now, that's uncalled for." Kendal spoke up. Huh, I wouldn't have expected him to stick up for me.

"No one was talking to you, dreads. So shut it." I watched the muscle in Kendal's cheek tighten in anger. A look I knew all too well. It was one he had often the last month of our relationship when I refused to give in to his request. I tried to catch his eye, but, like Rusty, he wouldn't look at me.

"Another word out of either of you, and I put a bullet in her." He turned us slightly so that I was facing the register again. "Where's the money?"

"In...in the drawer." The boy managed to stammer out.

"What the fuck?" He roared in my ear. "Are you stupid? Did you think I just wanted you to look at it? Put the fucking money in a bag and then stick it on the counter." There was a faint murmur from Mrs. Hill.

"Did you say something?" He directed at her. "I'm waiting, lady. Do you have something you want to say?"

"He's a child." She glared back at him. "You don't have to speak that way to him."

"Yea." Kendal murmured.

"What did I tell you people about talking?" He pressed the gun into my sweater, just above where his hand gripped my arm and fired. Heat radiated down my arm, and I couldn't contain my shocked scream.

"What the fuck?" Rusty yelled, taking a step in my direction.

"The next one goes in her head." Rusty skidded to a stop when the gun pressed against my temple, frozen in place as he put his hands in front of him in the classic surrender pose.

13

I could feel wetness on my palm, and looked down to find the white fabric of my sweater had turned crimson as blood flowed freely down my arm and into my clenched fist. When I opened my hand, the blood fell to the floor to join the droplets already there. I assumed they were from the initial blast of the bullet entering my flesh. The pain was surprisingly manageable, kinda like a stubbed toe. It throbbed now and then when my arm moved, but I could deal with it.

"Where the hell's my money?"

"On the counter." The teenager was pasty white and sweating profusely now.

"Bring it here." The man holding me ordered. "Fuck! You're getting blood on me." He gave me a shake that made the throbbing in my arm stronger. I managed to stifle my cry of pain by biting down on my lip. I was not going to give him the satisfaction of knowing that he was causing me more pain than he already had.

The kid made his way cautiously to where we stood. I couldn't say I blamed him. I wouldn't want to approach the guy who had just shot a woman because someone else had talked either. When he was arm's distance away, he held out the plastic shopping bag. The cash from the register barely came to the center of the pharmacy's logo on the bag.

"Where the fuck's the rest of it?"

"Th... that...that's all of it." The boy was back to stammering again.

"Fuck!" His angry shout echoed throughout the store. He released his hold on my arm long enough to snatch the bag from the boy.

Before I could even contemplate fleeing, he wrapped his forearm across my throat, bag in his hand, and pressed me tightly to his chest. The gun was still pressed against my temple, but I had both arms free now. Not like my left one would be much good at the moment, with the pressure of his hand gone, wave after wave of pain ran down my arm and up into my shoulder.

"Get on your knees." He ordered the others. When Mrs. Hill didn't move fast enough for his liking; he tapped the barrel of the pistol against my head. "Don't test my fucking patience. If you're not on the floor in ten seconds, her brains will be decorating this place."

I realized in horror that this crazy man was planning on taking me with him when he left, and there was a high probability that he was going to kill me when I had outlived my usefulness. Most likely, the moment we arrived at his getaway car. I had to do something. I wasn't ready for my life to end, not like this.

Chapter 3

THINK, AUTUMN THINK, I coached myself as I tried to focus on coming up with a plan and not reacting out of sheer panic. It was getting harder to concentrate as the seconds ticked by. I knew that at any moment the man holding me hostage would start to make his way to the door, taking my chances for survival with him.

I glanced over at Rusty; his eyes were focused on me now. Maybe I could get a message to him now that the gun wielding maniac could no longer see my face. Wait! He was smaller than me; he wouldn't be able to carry me out of here, and he wasn't that strong. If I could get Rusty on board with my plan, I might have a chance of getting out of this mess alive. I really hoped that Rusty could read lips.

"He's going to kill me." I mouthed the words as I looked at Rusty. He frowned at me, and I tried again, trying to form the words slowly. "He's going to kill me." When he didn't frown again, I moved on. "When he moves, I'm going to let all my weight fall on him. It should surprise him enough that he should drop me." Here was the tricky part. I wasn't sure if Rusty would be willing to risk his life for mine or not. "Can you... will you get the gun from him?"

Rusty didn't have time to figure out a way to respond; we started to move. The man holding me took one step back and then another, choking me when I didn't keep up with him. My knockoff boots had no traction, and my feet slid on the floor that was slick with my blood.

"If anyone tries to play fucking hero, they'll get a bullet to the chest, and so will she." The gun was still pressed against my temple. "See that clock." He used the gun to gesture to the clock on the wall behind the register. "You can get up and go about your lives after ten minutes have passed. Got it?"

I felt his weight shift as he went to take another step, and seized the opportunity. The gun wasn't pressed against me, so there was a good chance I wouldn't find a bullet lodged in my skull. I closed my eyes and let myself go limp. He had to support all of my weight with the one arm that was wedged around my throat. The pressure at my neck was uncomfortably tight for two seconds before my captor lost his balance and went sprawling backwards, with me on top of him. I heard the clatter of metal on the tile floor and opened one eye to see the gun come to a stop against a magazine rack just out of reach.

"Stupid bitch!" The man screamed as he kicked and pushed at me in his attempt to get away. I winced as one kick landed on my spine and couldn't help but cry out as his fingers dug into the wound left by the bullet. The edges of my world started to go dark as he untangled himself from me, and I watched in horror as he dove for the gun.

All I could see was the barrel of the gun, a black hole pointed straight at me. I knew that there would be no coming back once he pulled the trigger. At least I had tried. I hadn't given up without a fight. I closed my eyes again. I didn't want to watch the coming of my death.

The retort of the gun was deafening in the small space and I waited for the pain...that never came. Did death negate pain? I opened my eyes to look around and see what the afterlife held for me.

Rusty had the man pinned to the floor in front of me, his knee in the center of his back. He had his arms twisted behind him and secured in one large hand. With the other, he had the would-be thief's face ground into the blood stained tile. Kendal stood next to them, a different gun than the one that had been used on me, trained on the man beneath Rusty. Mrs. Hill let out a cry as I attempted to sit up.

"Are you okay, Autumn?" Kendal asked, giving me a sideways glance. Was he serious? I had been shot and used as a human shield. No, I wasn't okay, but as I looked over to where Mrs. Hill knelt on the floor I guessed I was okay. At least better than the teenage clerk who was now lying on the floor with a pool of blood spreading around him. "Autumn?" He prompted again, but I just stared in disbelief as Mrs. Hill attempted to use her handkerchief to staunch the flow of blood coming from the wound in the boy's chest.

"Help her." I whispered.

"I think..." Mrs. Hill's voice wavered as she spoke. "I think he's gone." She sat next to the body, staring at the blood staining her hands and dress. I wanted to comfort her, but it was taking everything I had to sit upright at the moment.

I could hear a siren in the distance, and I briefly wondered if anyone had thought to place a call to 911. My head felt so heavy and I was cold. I wished I had a blanket to curl up under as I gave in to my body's demands to lay down. I just needed to rest a moment, and then I'd get my phone out to call for help.

"Ma'am, can you hear me? Ma'am?" A feminine voice asked from nearby. It had a more youthful tone to it than Mrs. Hill, the only other woman in the store. I opened my eyes to find a paramedic kneeling next to me. "Can you tell me your name?" She asked when she noticed my eyes were open.

"Autumn."

"That's good, Autumn. Can you tell me where you're injured?"

"My arm. He shot me in the arm."

"Anywhere else?" She inquired, grabbing a roll of gauze from her bag.

"He kicked her pretty hard in the back and sides." Kendal interrupted. Out of the corner of my eye, I could see him standing off to the side, watching intently as the paramedic started to treat me.

"I'll need a collar." She yelled over her shoulder before returning her attention to my arm. "I'm not going to lie; this is probably going to hurt." She told me before she started to cut open the sleeve of my sweater.

I bit my lip to hold in my cry of pain as she peeled the fabric away from my arm. The blood had started to clot, attaching the frayed edges of the sweater to my skin. I watched as she examined the hole in my arm; fresh blood starting to trickle from the wound now that she had disturbed it.

The sound of Rusty's voice, raised in annoyance, distracted me from my current situation. He wasn't in my line of sight, and I wondered why he was getting upset. Tonight had definitely not gone as planned. In fact, it made the rest of the day seem like a good day. So much for my stress relief.

Before I could protest, a hard plastic collar was fastened around my neck, preventing me from moving my head more than a few inches in either direction, and a board was placed under my back. I was surrounded by six large men, three on either side, who used the handles on the board to lift me onto a gurney. I caught Rusty's eye as I was rolled by him. He was standing with a uniformed officer who had his back to me, and I assumed he was giving his statement. He held my gaze as I stared at him, suddenly feeling alone.

"Don't leave me there." I called to him before I could think better of it.

He gave a brief nod as I went through the door, and he was out of my line of sight. I couldn't be sure he had been responding to me or the officer that was with him, but I hoped it had been me. I didn't want to be alone at the hospital.

Chapter 4

THE INCESSANT BEEPING woke me from the light sleep I had fallen into after I had been placed in a room. I glanced at the clock on the wall to see I had only managed to sleep for a half hour.

"Sir. Sir, you can't go in there." A feminine voice insisted from just outside my door. "I'll have to call security if you can't follow the rules."

"I guess you'll have to do that then." Rusty said as he walked into my room.

"What did you do to piss off the nurse?" I asked him as he approached.

"She thinks I'm trouble." He shrugged, taking a seat in the chair next to the bed. "Plus, your boyfriend told her that he was the only one allowed in."

"What boyfriend?" My breath hissed through my teeth as I bumped my arm against the rail on the bed.

"The pretty boy from the store."

"Kendal is my ex. We haven't spoken in years." What game was Kendal playing at now? If he was so concerned about my wellbeing, why was he hiding out in the waiting room and not sitting next to my bed in the chair Rusty now occupied?

"That isn't the story he's telling."

"I think I have a say in who gets to visit me when I'm in the damn hospital. Which, is all your fault." I tacked on, my anger getting the better of me.

"How the hell is this my fault?" He crossed his impressive arms across his chest, cocking his head to the side in a silent challenge.

"If you had picked up the damn condoms before coming to get me, I wouldn't have been there."

"Do you really want to play this game tonight, Autumn?"

"No," I sighed in defeat. "I want to go home."

"Don't think that's going to happen. You lost consciousness multiple times tonight. They're going to keep you until at least morning."

"I can sign myself out."

"Oh? How are you going to get home?"

"You. Or a taxi." He laughed at that. We both knew that I'd have to call for a taxi from the next town over, and it would cost me at least fifty dollars to make it the ten miles back to my house. "I'll walk. I don't care. I'm not staying here."

"If you can convince them to let you leave, I'll get you home." The words were barely out of his mouth when I pressed the button to call for the nurse.

The nurse took her sweet time in answering my summons and glared at Rusty the entire time she explained to me why I couldn't just leave the hospital. I listened to her spiel politely before telling her that I didn't care about laws or the risks associated with leaving before they thought I was ready to do so. I would be leaving with or without permission within the next hour. The nurse huffed away after telling me she would be back with the doctor.

"That went well." Rusty smirked as the door closed.

"Where are my clothes?" I asked, ignoring his attempt to bait me.

"No clue. Possibly evidence."

"Fuck. This thing does not have the appropriate coverage for a ride on the back of your bike." I plucked the hospital gown away from my skin.

"If the doctor agrees to sign your release papers, I'll find you something to wear."

The smug look on his face disappeared a short time later when the doctor, reluctantly, gave in to my demands to be discharged from the hospital. My vitals were fine, and other than the hole in my arm, which had been stitched up, my injuries were minor. The kicks had left behind some nasty bruises, which I was told would get worse, but no broken bones or internal bleeding. The doctor shook his head as he walked away, promising to have my discharge paperwork ready to go in a half hour.

"Looks like you owe me some clothing." I told Rusty when we were alone again.

"I'll be back shortly." He grumbled as he left the room.

I waited impatiently for the return of my freedom. I hated feeling confined. Today could officially go down as the worst day of my life. No promotion. No sex. And I got shot. At least it was the weekend, and I had a few days before I had to face anyone again. I closed my eyes when I felt the tears starting to form. No way in hell was I going to end the day by crying.

I heard the door creak open and assumed it was Rusty when no perky voice announced itself. I sucked in a deep breath to fortify myself.

"Well, what did you come up with?"

"What are you talking about?"

"Kendal?" I was floored. What could he possibly be doing here? I thought Rusty had been making a joke when he mentioned him earlier.

"You were expecting someone else?"

"Of course. We haven't so much as waved hello to one another in well over ten years. What are you doing here?"

"You need someone to look after you. Especially after being shot tonight. I know it's not the right time, but when I saw him holding the gun to you... it changed everything. I couldn't let another minute pass without you being a part of my life again."

"I think..."

"You don't have to say anything now." He cut me off. "Not so soon after everything that's happened. I shouldn't have said anything either, but I couldn't wait. Not seeing you like this. I needed you to know that I still care."

"Blue or green?" Rusty asked, walking into the room. "Or am I interrupting something?"

"Your paperwork." The nurse stated as she followed along behind Rusty. Her previously perky tone is now aggravated. The small room was suddenly crowded, and it was more than I could take. I needed to get out of here. My head swam as I stood up quickly, and it took a moment before I didn't feel like the world was spinning. I snatched the clothing out of Rusty's hands on my way to the small, attached bathroom.

I locked the door behind me as I let the gown slide to the floor, my face heating up when I realized that I had flashed my ass to everyone in the room. I slipped on a green pair of scrub bottoms and a blue top that fit a little snugly but would work until I was home again. I left the bathroom without looking in the mirror; some things were better off not seeing.

The room was eerily quiet when I re-entered. It appeared that Rusty and Kendal were having a staring contest while the nurse hovered in the doorway, unsure of what action to take. I walked in between the two men, effectively ending their competition, to take my discharge papers from the nurse.

"Are you coming?" I asked over my shoulder before entering the hallway.

"Where are you going?" Kendal called after me.

"Home." Rusty responded for me, and I could hear the thump of his boots as he followed me to the elevators.

Chapter 5

I WAS SHIVERING BY the time I walked through my front door. Scrubs definitely provided very little protection against the night air. Although, we had made it home in record time. Turns out there's no traffic at two in the morning.

"Do you want me to stay?" Rusty called from the driveway. "I'll be fine." I shut the door behind me before he could respond. I glanced at the stairs leading to my bedroom and then at the sofa, waiting a few feet away, and decided it wasn't worth the effort to climb the stairs. Plus, there would be less chance of rolling over and inflicting more pain on myself on the sofa.

The chime of the doorbell pulled me from sleep, and I cursed whoever was responsible for pressing it. The sun was still peeking through the front windows, which meant that it was before noon. My arm ached, as did the rest of my body. There didn't seem to be a part of me that didn't hurt. The bell chimed again as I debated ignoring it. Whoever was out there sure was persistent. I hobbled to the front door, wrapping my good arm around my ribs in an attempt to keep them from hurting every time I took a step.

Kendal was standing on the front stoop, one arm cradling a bouquet of roses and the other raised to ring the bell again.

"Hi," he said bashfully when I glared at him from the doorway.

"What are you doing here?" I knew my tone was harsh, but I wasn't in the mood to play games with my ex.

"Checking on you."

"Why? We haven't said a single word to one another in years."

"That's my fault." He paused. "Let me come in so we can talk in private."

"I don't think we have anything more to say to one another. You made your choice when you left."

"Why are you always so damn difficult?" Kendal pushed his dreads back from his face in frustration. I'd seen that move a hundred times or more at the end of our relationship. He hadn't been able to understand why I wouldn't sit around and wait for him to come back to me while he went out and explored his sexuality with other people.

"I'm trying to save us both a headache." One that I could already feel forming behind my left eye. When he just stared me down, I gave in. It would be easier to hear what he had to say now rather than have him come back later. "Fine, come in." I gestured for him to enter and had to hold back a gasp of pain from moving my injured arm.

I admired his swimmer's physique as he glided by me into the house, and enjoyed the fact that Kendal only seemed to improve with age, unlike the majority of our peers who had let their bodies start to go soft. I reminded myself that this was the man who had broken my heart and that I was only letting him into my home to get rid of him faster.

I trailed behind him to the living room where he sat on the sofa I had just vacated. I remembered this move from college and chose to take a seat across from him in the rocking chair. I didn't want to have my personal space invaded this morning. When he frowned, I knew that I had made the proper decision.

"Don't you want to sit somewhere more comfortable, given your injuries?"

"I'm fine where I am, Kendal. Now what was so important that it couldn't wait until later in the day?"

"How are you?"

"Are you serious right now? How do you think I am? I've been home for less than twelve hours after being held hostage and shot."

"Calm down, Autumn. That's why I'm here. You've been through a traumatic experience and shouldn't be left alone. I'm not surprised that the biker ditched you as soon as he could. Why on earth would you even associate with trash like that? He can't possibly do anything but drag you down."

I was livid by the time the last word left his mouth. "Get out." I said quietly. I wouldn't argue or cause a scene like I had when I was younger. I had grown since then, well enough to know that I didn't have the energy to throw a full-blown tantrum like I wanted to. How dare he try to tell me who to associate with. Like his opinion meant anything to me anymore. Kendal had lost any influence on my opinions the day he told me he wanted to take a break for a few months so he could experience what it was like to be with another man. When he wanted me to say that I was okay with him cheating on me. The day he told me that I wasn't what he wanted in a partner.

"What? Why?" His lower lip stuck out in what I used to refer to his puppy dog look. Big, brown eyes staring back at me in mock sorrow.

"Because I don't want you here." I stood up. "Now, please leave. Like you said, I've been through a traumatic experience and need to rest."

"Which is why I should stay with you." Kendal protested as I started to walk to the front door.

"I'm fine on my own." I opened the door.

"I miss you, Auty." He whispered as he stood up.

"You have a funny way of showing it." Rusty laughed as he walked through the door.

"What the hell are you doing here?" Kendal demanded.

"Checking on Autumn, and it looks like I arrived just in time to take out some trash. Do you want to do this the easy way or the hard way, pretty boy?" Rusty cracked his knuckles as he spoke.

"You have no authority here. This isn't your concern." Kendal set the flowers he'd been holding all this time on the sofa and rolled his shoulders as he took a step toward Rusty.

"I believe it became my concern when Autumn asked you to leave and you refused."

"Disagreements in relationships are normal. So why don't you go back to drinking and whoring and allow us to finish our conversation like civilized adults?" I couldn't contain my snort when he referred to us having a relationship, but quickly regretted my inability to do so. The pain that shot through my ribs was intense.

Rusty threw me a concerned look before crossing the room to stand next to Kendal. "Listen here, Kenny-boy; your relationship with Autumn ended years ago when you left. The entire town knows it, even if you don't. So why don't you do yourself a favor and leave now before you embarrass yourself even further? I'll even help you." Rusty tossed one of his muscular arms around Kendal's shoulders and started to guide him to the door. By the look on Kendal's face, I could only guess that Rusty was applying pressure when he tried to resist.

"Autumn," Kendal implored. "Why are you letting him do this to us?"

"There is no us. I'm not sure why you suddenly seem to think that there is, but you need to leave now."

"You nearly died last night."

"That doesn't change anything. Goodbye, Kendal." I shut the door as he opened his mouth to speak again and turned to face my other visitor. "What are you doing here?"

"I figured you'd be ready to have your ribs re-wrapped after a night of sleep." He pulled a roll of gauze from his jacket and latched a finger onto the bottom of my scrub top.

Chapter 6

"I CAN DO IT MYSELF." I protested as Rusty followed me up the stairs.

"Just because you can doesn't mean you should. Besides, it's highly unlikely that you'll be able to get the bandage tight enough to isolate your ribs properly. It's not like I haven't seen you naked before, so I don't understand what the big deal is." Rusty stopped at my bedroom door, as though he needed permission to enter.

I would be stupid to pretend that I knew the proper way to wrap my ribs. This was the first serious injury I'd ever sustained if you didn't count the time I broke my little toe in college. Based on the scars I'd seen on Rusty's body, it was clear he had more experience with bruised ribs than I did.

"Well, are you going to help me or not?" I was irritated with Rusty but more so with myself as Rusty just watched me grimace as I took off the scrub top from the doorway.

He moved with a silent swiftness I hadn't witnessed from him before, a look of determination on his face. It was as if his entire body was on alert while he focused on the task at hand, like he had crossed into enemy territory. It was a brief glimpse into the man that everyone else knew as Diablo, and it was gone as quickly as it appeared.

"This will probably hurt." He said as he started to unravel the gauze that had begun to sag. "But it will feel better when the new bandage is on." I focused on the play of muscles across his chest as he worked. It helped distract me from the sharp ache I felt every time I drew a breath. I was surprised when the ache began to diminish as he wound the new bandage around my chest. I hadn't really believed that something as simple as a roll of gauze would help to relieve the pain.

"All done." Rusty said, taking a step back. "If you were one of the guys, I'd give you a smack on the back to prove the quality of my work, but I think we can forgo it this time." He grinned as he looked down at my topless form.

"Smooth." I muttered turning away to grab the tank top laying across the foot end of my bed, but before I could put it on, I got distracted by the image that my vanity mirror displayed. Not that of the ruggedly handsome, if not a bit scary looking, man standing by my bed, but by the bruised and bloody picture I presented. My right side was a mass of dark blues and deep purples; the bandage on my arm looked a little worse for the wear. There was dried blood on my arm, in my hair, and even some on my face. Not to mention the dark circles under my eyes. Why hadn't someone mentioned my disturbing appearance to me? Hell, why hadn't the hospital offered to help me clean up better?

Maybe they would have if you hadn't insisted on signing yourself out in the middle of the night, I chided myself.

"Problem?" Rusty asked, catching my eye in the mirror.

"No. Just taking stock of my injuries." I admitted pulling the shirt over my head. I had to hold back a hiss of pain. Apparently, my arm had decided to make its displeasure known too. Everything hurt as I slowly lowered my arms, hoping the slower movement would hurt less. No such luck. It was like getting kicked in the ribs all over again.

"You should probably stick to button-up shirts for a while." He added helpfully.

"Good time to tell me that." I grumbled. Not like I owned any of those. My shoulders were too broad for them to fit properly.

My stomach grumbled audibly just as the doorbell rang. Great, just what I needed, more unwanted company. I debated not answering the door and decided a quick look out my bedroom window was in order. It was my mother, which meant that she wouldn't just go away if I ignored her. She'd continue to ring the bell until I answered the door. Don't get me wrong, I loved my mother, but some days she was just a pain in my butt.

"Stay here." I demanded as the doorbell chimed again.

Chapter 7

"IT TOOK YOU LONG ENOUGH. Were you still in bed?" My mother bustled through the doorway, the scent of White Diamonds trailing behind her. Although her words held a note of censure, her tone was curious, and I waited patiently until she got to the reason behind her visit. If I had to guess, it was because she had already heard about the attempted robbery.

I followed her slowly into the kitchen where she was pulling mugs out of the cupboard to prepare tea, the kettle already on the stove top. My mother wasted no time on getting what she wanted, and even though I had no desire to sit in the kitchen and drink tea this morning while rehashing my previous evening, that's exactly what I would be doing.

"I was upstairs changing."

"You should have showered first. You look a little rough around the edges." She deftly scooped the kettle off the stove as it started to whistle.

"Thanks, mom."

"You know I don't sugarcoat things." She brought the mugs to the table and took a seat. Then stared me down until I gingerly copied her and accepted my mug of tea. "I added honey to help sweeten you up some." She smiled before taking a sip of the still steaming liquid. "Now then, why am I the last to know that my daughter was involved in a robbery last night and ended up in the hospital?" Her voice quavered a bit on the last word.

"It was late when I left the hospital, and I didn't want to wake you up in the middle of the night when it could wait until today. My injuries weren't severe enough to warrant you worrying over me." I played with the mug in front of me as I spoke, trying to relieve the nervous energy running through my body. My mother would throw a fit of epic proportions if she found Rusty in my house.

"It's never too late to tell your mother that you're okay." She used the mom stare on me. The one, that as a child, could make me feel guilty enough to confess to sins I hadn't even committed just to make her stop.

I shook my head; I was an adult now. I had nothing to feel guilty about. In fact, I was the victim of this entire mess. Why wasn't she fawning over me? Making sure I was resting comfortably and had everything I needed.

"Who told you about the robbery?" I asked in an attempt to take control of the conversation. If I could get her to talk about last night's events and fill in details that the town gossips wouldn't know, she would drop the guilt trip she was trying to lay on me.

"I had several text messages this morning when I woke up, and Kendal came to the house a little before eight." That rotten bastard. "I don't know why you won't give him a second chance.

He's polite and respectful, not to mention easy on the eyes." I stifled a groan. I was not going to touch that remark with a ten foot pole.

"Kendal was busy this morning." I remarked taking a sip of the tea to stop the rant I could feel building.

"I was expecting him to still be here when I arrived. I waited to come over so that you two could have some alone time. Especially since you let that awful biker you've apparently been hanging around with take you home last night. Honestly, Autumn, what are you thinking? I know I raised you better than that." She practically spat the word biker, like it left a bad taste in her mouth.

"That biker is my friend. Who you also happen to know. Remember Rusty? The little boy who grew up in the house next to us? Yea, that's the 'awful biker' I let take me home last night. He's been a better friend to me than Kendal ever was."

"There's no need to get hostile about it." She chided. "Who would have ever thought that sweet little boy would grow up to be a thug?"

"He is not a thug." I defended the man hiding in my bedroom. You treat him like he's one, though; the little voice in the back of my head taunted. Not good enough to be seen with in public. Enough! I silenced the voice. I would deal with my confusing thoughts and feelings towards Rusty later.

"If he's not a thug, then what does he do for a living?" My mother looked superiorly over the rim of her mug.

"What does that have to do with anything? Your job does not make you a good person. Just like riding a motorcycle doesn't

41

make you a bad person. Both things are just part of who you are and what you're interested in."

"Pretty words dear, but it still doesn't change the fact that if he doesn't have a job, he's not a contributing member of society, which makes him a thug." Argh! She was so frustrating some days. Like a dog with a bone, she wouldn't drop the subject until I admitted that she was right.

"He's a mechanic." It wasn't a complete lie; I had seen him work on the bikes parked around his place a few times.

"Well," she sniffed, "there are worse occupations."

It was funny how judgmental my mom could be when she had been a housewife her entire life. After my father passed away, she had moved to a smaller home closer to town and started hanging out with the other widows. Playing bridge and bingo, taking trips to the casino with the other retirees, and getting her hair done once a week at the salon. She had taken pleasure in sharing town gossip with anyone that would listen, and normally she was harmless, but today she was working on my last nerve. "I should go back to resting, mom." I told her before I got up from the table to dump my still full mug of now tepid tea down the drain. "You're welcome to stay and play nurse, but I'll probably sleep most of the day."

She joined me at the sink, her familiar scent wafting around me comfortingly. "Well, if you're sure you'll be okay. I was planning on attending bingo today with the girls. I'll have my cell phone with me if you need me."

"I'll be fine. I love you, mom." I told her. It was one of the few times I was glad we weren't a demonstrative family. Leaning down to hug her would have hurt more than I would have been able to hide.

"I love you too, Autumn." She patted my uninjured arm and showed herself out.

I rinsed out the tea mugs, wasting time in the kitchen before I headed back upstairs to face Rusty. When the kitchen was back in order, I slowly limped my way back up to my bedroom, which was empty. Where the hell was he?

Not in the mood to play games, I sat on my bed, which made an odd crinkling noise when I sat. I reached under my legs and fished around. My fingers brushed against something that produced the noise again, and I was surprised when I pulled out a small scrap of paper.

Close the window. I'll check in later.

Chapter 8

IF ANYTHING, I FELT even more broken and bruised when I woke up Sunday morning. I groaned like a little old lady as I got out of bed and shuffled my way to the bathroom; everything ached. I cursed out loud when I realized the bandages holding me together had sagged during the night. No wonder everything hurt.

After I showered, I attempted to wrap my ribs back up. I knew that the bandage wasn't as tight as Rusty had made it the day before, but it would do, I hoped. Next up, groceries. I had no real desire to leave the house, but I needed to eat. This wasn't a child's tale. There was no fairy godmother that would bring me food while woodland creatures cleaned my home. So, facing the world it was.

Baggy clothing hid my bandages, and a handful of painkillers dulled the ache enough to move without wincing. I knew that within minutes of being seen out of my house, everyone in town would be on the hunt for gossip. I would be the topic of conversation for days to come, unless something more shocking occurred first. Not that I wished anything bad to befall the residents of my small town, but if Evelyn just happened to get caught stealing from the company coffers, I wouldn't be sad.

I took my time and turned the five-minute drive to the grocery store into twelve; I wasn't taking chances. I could only imagine the pain I'd be in if I had to slam on the brakes. The store was relatively empty, thanks to the ongoing church services. For a small town, Ivory boasted two non-denominational churches, a Roman Catholic Cathedral, a mosque, and a Church of Faith. No matter what part of town you were in, you were never more than a few blocks away from a place of worship.

I managed to avoid the other customers in the store until I reached the checkout line. Apparently Sunday mornings weren't considered to be a prime grocery shopping time because Luca's Groceries only had one register running. There was a backup at the lone register as a mother with a crying infant and hyper toddler unloaded her overflowing cart. Two older gentlemen with baskets chatted together as they waited behind her, and I got in line behind them.

"How are you this morning, Autumn?" Kendal's familiar voice washed over me. I couldn't believe my lack of luck. I'd gone years without running into him, and now I'd seen him three times in as many days.

"Are you stalking me?" I demanded in a hushed tone.

"When did you get so dramatic? Jeez, Autumn, I'm doing the same thing you're doing. Buying groceries at the only store in town that's open on a Sunday." There was a heat in his voice that caused me to pause, like he was angry with me. What possible

46

reason could he have to be angry with me? I was the victim here, not him. "Is it so hard to believe that I still care about your wellbeing?"

I relented, just a little. "Thank you for your concern. I'll survive, but I'd prefer to go back to the way things were before Friday. Where we live in the same town and ignore one another. I was happy with that arrangement, weren't you?"

"No."

"Next." The cashier interrupted.

I chose to ignore his answer and loaded my purchases on the counter. When I had paid for my groceries and had placed the last bag in my cart, I turned to face him. "Goodbye, Kendal."
I walked out of Luca's hoping that he would remember and understand the meaning behind my words. Goodbye was final; I only said it when that part of my life was over. It was the first time I had said it to Kendal. When we had broken up, I hadn't expected him to actually leave. I had thought he would come to his senses, but he had left me without a backward glance. Now it was my turn to leave without looking back.

MONDAY DAWNED GRAY and blustery with rain threatening to fall at any moment. My ribs ached more than ever, but at least the rest of me hurt less. I was dreading going into work for the first time in sixteen years. Today was the first day of training my new boss, Evelyn, in a position that should have been mine. But that was water under the bridge at this point; I just needed to move forward.

My morning continued on the same path as the weekend, completely unexpected. Evelyn showed up two hours late and then told me that my help wouldn't be required. Twenty minutes later, an attractive man with piercing blue eyes and dark hair arrived on our floor. He knocked on Evelyn's office door briefly and then slipped into her office; the door clicked softly shut behind him. I continued to work on my report until my cell rang. The police requested my presence during my lunch hour, and I decided that I didn't need to interrupt Evelyn and her guest with that information.

By the time I made my way out of the building, the dark-haired man had been installed behind a desk outside of Evelyn's office with a plaque that read Administrative Assistant. My old boss hadn't required an assistant, and I wondered how much of her actual job Evelyn would be doing. If I had to take a guess, it would be none.

The police station bustled with activity, which surprised me. Ivory was a small town with a low crime rate, and yet there was only one empty seat in the waiting area, and several men and a woman were cuffed to the metal benches behind the reception desk. Thankfully, once I gave my name, I was escorted to a conference room at the back of the station and didn't need to take up residence next to the larger man in stained jeans, who had the faint aroma of manure wafting from him.

As I waited for the detective to join me, I peeked through the cracked door to the hallway beyond. I had never been in a police station before and didn't plan on making any return trips, so this was my one chance to see what the shows on television didn't show. It was rather boring, uniformed officers with paperwork, one with a sandwich, and a short woman in a pantsuit who rushed by so quickly I only realized she was a female when I saw the black leather heels. Then I heard the rumble of a voice I recognized, Rusty. What was he doing here?

His voice grew louder as he approached the room I was waiting in, and it wasn't long before his scuffed boots and well-worn jeans appeared in the small sliver of space I could see. I strained to hear his muffled words, but from where I was seated, I couldn't make out what was being said. So I just enjoyed the view. Rusty was an enticing male specimen, and it wasn't often that I got to observe him without his knowledge. The ripple of his muscles under the black t-shirt that was molded to his body, made me regret that we hadn't made it to his bed Friday night.

"I'll be in touch." Rusty's voice interrupted my lascivious thoughts of how the previous weekend should have played out.

"Have a good day, sir."

Sir? When did the police in Ivory become so polite when addressing what the town considered to be lower class citizens? Not that I saw Rusty as being lower class, but it was the general consensus of Ivory's residents that bikers were beneath them.

"Ms. Simon? I'm Detective Perry."

"Nice to meet you. Please call me Autumn."

"This should be relatively quick. I just need to take your statement about the events that occurred on Friday evening."

"Is that what Rusty was doing here, giving his statement?" I couldn't resist asking.

"I'm not at liberty to discuss the reason behind Mr. Peters' visit."

Chapter 9

I RETURNED TO WORK a few minutes after my allotted lunch hour and found Evelyn waiting at my desk. Great, just who I wanted to deal with after being interrogated for forty-five minutes. Somehow, my statement had turned into being questioned about everything I said. To the point that I wasn't sure if I was remembering events correctly. It was a disconcerting feeling, but I had nothing to hide.

"Where were you? You weren't in the company cafeteria." Evelyn demanded, her delicate eyebrows raised in exaggeration.

"I can leave company property for my lunch hour." I put my purse in my desk drawer before turning to face her. "Was there something I could help you with?"

"We need to discuss company policies and your understanding of them." She huffed.

"Which policies are you referring to?" The only thing I'd done was take a longer lunch by six minutes, which I already planned to make up this afternoon.

"Those about personal relationships." What in the world was she talking about? "As you know, this is a place of business, not a dating show. We can't have your suitors showing up at all hours looking for you. And another thing, I am not your secretary. Going forward, please conduct all personal business before or after the workday."

"I'm sorry. I don't understand what you're talking about."

"Your dreaded lover stopped by with some flowers, which I had Eric dispose of since we are an allergen-free building." Since when? "He was quite rude, demanding that he see you. I had him escorted off the premises."

"Thank you, Evelyn. If it wouldn't be too much trouble, could he be placed on the banned list?" My normally low-pitched voice raised an octave in fake sweetness. "He's an ex that seems to be having trouble understanding the meaning of the word." My response seemed to stop her in her tracks. Good, it was about time I got a leg up on her.

"Eric! Get his name from Autumn." Evelyn demanded and turned away, dismissing me.

The rest of my day went much smoother once Evelyn was safely ensconced back in her office, and before I knew it, the day was over. Both the E's had vacated the building an hour before my normal quitting time, which didn't surprise me one bit. I checked my phone as I walked to my car. Two missed calls from my mother and one from Kendal. I was sure I could figure out who had given him my number with one guess: my mother. I had changed it a few years ago, so it wasn't like he had saved it for all these years. I chose to ignore the voicemails for the time being and drove home.

My thoughts wandered back to what Rusty had been doing at the police station earlier in the day. He had talked to the police on Friday night, and he didn't seem like the type to voluntarily pay a visit to Ivory's finest. Detective Perry had been rather abrupt when I had asked him if Rusty had been giving a statement as well, which only raised more questions. I was a victim of the crime, so shouldn't I know more details about the case? Instead, I had been questioned and treated more like a criminal, which seemed odd to me. Especially the questions about Rusty's involvement in the night's events. Maybe Rusty had said something about us being there together, and the detective was trying to ascertain whether or not he was telling the truth. Which still didn't explain why I was politely but firmly informed that the reason for Rusty's visit to the station was none of my business.

Speak, or in this case, think of the devil, and he shall appear. Rusty was seated on the steps of my front porch when I pulled into my driveway. There was no reason for him to visit me, and my heart sped up just a bit in anticipation. We were only friends with benefits, and there were no benefits to be had at the moment. Could his visit mean something more?

Don't be one of those silly women that thinks the guy she's sleeping with has caught feelings! He probably saw you at the station today and wanted to check in with you. My inner voice chided as I approached him.

"How are the ribs?" He called out looking like sin on a stick. His muscled arms were bare, and the black t-shirt was more of a tease than a covering.

"Meh. You going to sit there all day or move so we can go inside?" He followed me into the house without a word.

"What were you doing down at the station today?" I asked, not shying away from the question that had been burning in my mind on my drive home.

"Got called down to clarify parts of my statement." He responded not missing a beat. "Heard you and that boy went grocery shopping together yesterday. I don't poach on other's territory, so I guess our arrangement is over."

"Are you fucking kidding me?" I was outraged. My ex was practically stalking me, and now Rusty was breaking up with me. "I don't share Autumn, you know that." He crossed his arms over his chest, and I almost got distracted by the way his muscles flexed, almost.

"There's nothing to share. I told you it was over. Apparently I'm the only one who understands that fact. Hell, today I got him banned from entering my place of employment. I'm not sure how much clearer I can be. If you don't trust me, then maybe we should just end this now!" I shouted. I'd had enough of men trying to tell me what to do.

"Calm down." His words were like a red flag being waved in front of a bull.

"Don't tell me what to do. We're just sleeping together, fucking. Isn't that what you told Detective Perry? Which doesn't give you any say over what I say and do. So you can just show yourself out now. We're done!"

Chapter 10

THERE WERE TEARS IN my eyes as I turned away and waited for the sound of Rusty's footsteps to fade and my front door to close. My shoulders tensed as he finally started to move. Hold it together girl, I sniffled to myself. Only a few more seconds and I could let the tears flow freely. I wasn't even sure why I was crying. We were friends with benefits, fuck buddies as he had so crudely put it to the detective, not partners in a committed relationship. We had no long-term future together. I knew this had only been a temporary arrangement, and I had been the one to end it. So, score one for me, right? A hand on my shoulder startled me from my bitter thoughts.

"Don't cry." He turned me to face him, and I quickly swiped at my damp cheeks.

"I'm not." I denied.

"I trust you. I was giving you an easy out. Which you can still take, and I won't be offended. The cat's out of the bag now, and people are going to talk about our relationship."

"Since when do you care about what people say?" I blinked back a fresh wave of tears.

"I don't. I care about how it will make you feel." This was new. The Rusty I knew didn't talk about the serious stuff; in fact, he avoided it at all costs. It was like I had stepped into an alternate reality where the man I was seeing actually discussed feelings instead of ignoring them and making jokes instead.

I stared at his chest. "I've never cared about what the small-minded people of this town have thought."

"You realize that if we continue this, we're going public, as in dates and holding hands. And..." He paused, as if unsure he should continue. "I'm going to deal with that ex of yours once and for all. He needs to learn that when a woman says no, it means you leave her alone." His hands still rested on my shoulders, and I found myself comforted by his closeness.

"So you're saying that you want a real relationship?" I was confused. When had weekly hookups turned into feelings? I knew that I had started to question how I felt about Rusty, but I was a woman; we were prone to do these things. Men, especially macho men that went by the name Diablo, didn't even admit to having feelings let alone initiate conversations about them.

"With all the bells and whistles, Autumn." I stared up at his face in disbelief. He wasn't joking.

"Why now?"

"I had a lot of time to think after I dropped you off Saturday morning. I was forced to stand by and watch as some crackhead held a gun to you and was helpless to do anything when he first shot and then attacked you. I hated pretending that I didn't know you when the police arrived, but it wasn't until I got to the hospital and was denied entrance to your room by that pretty boy," he sneered the words. "That I realized I wanted more from our relationship. I wanted to be able to claim you as my own."

I opened my mouth to protest his use of the word claim, but he pressed his finger against my lips. "Shh, you know what I mean. I don't want to hide our relationship anymore. I care about you and want to be able to take care of you when you need me."

"I care about you too, Rusty." I admitted.

"But do you want the rest?" Of course, admitting my feelings wouldn't satisfy him. It was time to make a decision. Did I want to be with a man who the rest of the world knew as Diablo? Did we have a future together? Could we have a future together? What if the relationship we had now was all we were meant to be? Ugh! I could play the what if game all day and not come up with an answer. Sometimes you don't need to know the answer at the beginning. You just needed the willingness to try.

"Yes, I want to be with you." And sealed the start of our new relationship with a kiss.

Chapter 11

THE REST OF THE WEEK passed slower than I hoped it would. I had my first real date with Rusty on Friday night, and it was only Thursday. He had warned me that he would be busy most of the week when he left Tuesday morning, and that I probably wouldn't hear from him until our date. And he was true to his word so far, not even a single text message. It was like nothing had changed.

I walked across the parking lot to my car, my thoughts preoccupied with my upcoming date with Rusty and what I should wear. So preoccupied that I didn't notice Kendal leaning against the concrete support beam next to my car until I was next to him. He looked angry, a scowl marring his handsome face.

"That snooty bitch had me banned from the building. How am I supposed to surprise you with a romantic dinner if I have to wait for you in the parking lot, like some second class citizen? I feel dirty just hanging out down here."

Well, at least he didn't know that I was the one who had him banned. But why was he trying to surprise me with a romantic dinner? I thought he had finally got the message that I wasn't interested in rekindling our failed relationship when I didn't contact him. Instead, he was still trying; I didn't remember him being this persistent. Maybe he thought I was playing hard to get.

"Kendal, it's over. Why are you still trying?" I tried to keep the frustration out of my voice.

"Why won't you give me a chance?"

"I did that before, and you broke my heart. I've found someone new."

"Who? That biker." He scoffed. "I can provide you with a better life than he ever could."

"I don't need anyone to give me anything. I need someone that I can count on, someone that I can trust to be there for me." Kendal crossed his arms across his chest and leaned back against the wall.

"I was always there for you."

"Until I wasn't enough for you." I interrupted him. "Then you distanced yourself from me and finally ended things when I wouldn't give in to your request."

"You were always enough for me. I just needed to experiment before I was ready to settle down. I needed to explore all life had to offer." He huffed out a breath and pulled his hair away from his neck.

"What's to stop you from needing another exploration period? Nothing." I answered for him.

"Can we not have this conversation here?" He gestured widely and drew in a deep breath. "In a parking lot. We're not teenagers. This is an adult conversation that should take place in private."

"Fine." I relented. We would have this conversation, and then I could move on. Closing this chapter in my life for good. "How about we go to that dinner you had planned? As friends only." I clarified quickly when I saw his eyes start to light up.

"I'll drive." He stopped my words of protest by rushing on. "It will be easier on us both, and when dinner is over, I can bring you back here to your car."

"Fine." I relented and quickly added. "I want to be home by nine. I'm still recovering and need my rest."

"If you insist." Kendal tipped his head and started across the parking lot to his car.

I had flashbacks to high school when I got in the passenger seat of Kendal's car. Even though it was a newer model, it still smelled the same; clove cigarettes and Black Ice air freshener. We headed toward the north end of town, and I got confused when we turned onto a road that led out-of-town.

"I thought we were staying in town. Where are we going?"

"It's a surprise."

"You know I hate surprises." Now it was my turn to huff. We pulled into the driveway of an outdated brick home a few minutes later. "Where are we?"

"My house."

"I never agreed to come to your house." I practically yelled.

"You never asked where dinner was. Come on, I'm not going to bite you. We both know that's your thing, not mine." Kendal grinned and left me sitting in his car stunned.

How the hell did I keep finding myself in these situations? One moment it was a normal day, and the next I found myself in a waking nightmare. I contemplated calling Rusty to come get me, but I was a big girl and could take care of myself. I would listen to what Kendal had to say, get a free meal, and then move on with my life. I had a date to prepare for, so the sooner I got out of the car, the sooner I could be home picking out an outfit.

The inside of Kendal's house was dark, lit only by candle light with dark blue walls that didn't reflect the light. It looked like the candles had been burning for quite a while. I was starting to have second thoughts until I peeked into what I assumed was the living room and saw real light fixtures. I was still reluctant to leave the entrance hall, though.

"Do you want me to blow out the candles?" I called out, still unsure of where Kendal had disappeared to.

He popped his head out of a doorway toward the back of the hall. "They're fine. You can join me back here in the kitchen."

The deeper I walked into the house, the more uneasy I became. This definitely wasn't one of my brightest ideas. No one knew where I was or who I was with. The sooner I listened to what Kendal had to say, the faster I could get back to my car and to the safety of my home.

"I thought you would have outgrown the dark phase by now." I commented as I stepped into the kitchen. The walls were the same dark blue as the rest of the house, and the countertops were a black granite. Shiny black appliances gleamed in the startling bright light of the fluorescent bulbs in the overhead lights.

Kendal shrugged in response. "Dinner will be ready in a minute. Since you want a friendly dinner, we can eat here in the kitchen at the bar. Unless you've had a change of heart."

"The bar will be fine." I replied as I looked around the room to see what bar he was talking about. Tucked in the corner was a counter with two bar stools. Above the counter was a folding shutter, which I assumed opened up to the dining room.

"Have a seat. I'll bring our food over." Kendal said, focused on putting the finishing touches on our meal, which I had to admit smelled good, even though I wasn't sure what it was.

I waited awkwardly by the stools for Kendal to join me. It was unbelievably tempting to fall into old routines and tease him about his cooking skills. He had been the one to do the cooking when we were together, and I had teased him relentlessly about being the girl in the relationship. But the time for teasing had passed; we were strangers now.

Kendal brought over plates of beef roast with potatoes and carrots covered in a thick brown gravy, interrupting my wayward thoughts. "Enjoy."

"Thank you." I accepted the plate and waited for Kendal to take a seat before joining him.

"So..." We both started and I laughed nervously at our old habit of speaking at the same time.

"Go ahead." I said taking a bite. He was the one that wanted to talk, after all.

"I just want to know why you're so adamantly against giving us another chance." Nothing like getting straight to the point. Might as well return the favor.

"You broke my heart. You were the one person I thought I could count on to always be there for me, and then you asked me to accept the fact that you wanted to experiment with other men and possibly group sex. It was a slap in the face. That request was you telling me that I wasn't enough for you, that I wasn't good enough. And you refused to even consider why I would be hurt by your actions. You were selfish." Kendal started to protest but I forged ahead. "You lost my trust the day you told me that you had spent the night with a guy you met at the bar. You don't do that to someone you love. You don't spend the night with someone else and expect them to understand what you did because you call it an experiment. That's not love, not even close."

"You're right. I'm sorry." The words were a few years too late in being said. "I still care about you, Auty." The pet name nearly brought tears to my eyes.

"I know you want me to say that I care for you too, but I can't. It would be a lie."

"What if I asked for your friendship?"

"Maybe we could try to be friends again."

"That's how we started." He picked sadly at his food now. "As friends." Kendal's voice was barely above a whisper, and my heart ached with regret.

"We can try." I pushed my plate away from me.

"So friend, how have you been coping with what happened last Friday?" Umm... hello change of topic!

"Okay, I guess." I wasn't sure what had just happened. The glum Kendal was gone, and in his place was a decidedly more cheerful person, almost happy. "Most of it is just a blur now, which is probably for the best."

"But not all of it?"

"No, I can remember the moments leading up to being accosted with crystal clarity. It wasn't until he pulled the gun on me that things start to blend together."

"Do you want dessert? Or wine?" Kendal asked as he collected our plates.

"A glass of wine would be nice."

I sipped from the glass slowly as Kendal went about cleaning up the kitchen. It had been such an unusual evening. After years of waiting, I got to say all the things I wanted to say to Kendal, and I did it without getting emotional. I guess I really was over him once and for all.

"Ready to go back to your car?" Kendal asked suddenly standing next to me.

"Yes." I had a hard time getting the word out of my mouth. I stood up slowly and sat back down as the room started to spin. I only had one glass of wine; if anything, I should be tipsy, not drunk. I stood again and shook my head in an attempt to clear it. I started to follow Kendal to the front of the house and hoped that fresh air would help to sober me up.

Halfway down the hall, I crashed into the wall and nearly knocked a candle from its holder on the wall. "I think I need a moment."

"You're going to need more than that." Kendal said his words sounded muffled. He opened one of the closed doors and ushered me inside. "I'm sorry about this Autumn, but you insisted on doing things the hard way. I wish things could have been different."

"I...don't...under...stand." It took all my concentration to say such a simple sentence.

"I drugged your wine." He lowered me to what felt like a sofa, but the room was dark and my eyes kept closing. "You admitted that you remember everything that happened before that idiot took you hostage, and that just won't work for me." His voice came from farther away, and I forced myself to open my eyes.

"I truly am sorry." He said as he closed the door behind him.

Chapter 12

EVERYTHING HURT, AND my mouth felt like it had been stuffed with cotton balls all night long. The ache in my head, for the first time in what felt like forever, was worse than that of my ribs. I sat up and tried to figure out where I was. I knew I wasn't in my room. My bedroom had windows that let in light from the outside, and this room was pitch black.

Ok, Autumn, what's the last thing you remember? I asked myself as I checked for any new sore spots. Thankful to discover all my clothing seemed to be in place while I checked for injuries.

I had gone to dinner with Kendal. Wait, that was wrong. I agreed to go to dinner with him, and he had brought me back to his house. We had dinner, and I had told him why we could never be together. We had talked about Friday night and then... things started to get blurry. I had a glass of wine, maybe more? But why would I have more than one glass of wine after dinner? What happened after the wine? What did we do? My car; we were going back to my car and I got sick. No, not sick. Kendal admitted to drugging me and then put me in here.

That bastard! I knew I couldn't trust him. Where was my purse? I couldn't feel it as I felt around me on the sofa I had passed out on. It was mostly wishful thinking on my part that he would have actually left my purse with me. My phone was in my purse, and I would have been able to call for help. I wasn't sure what Kendal was planning, but it couldn't be good if he thought he needed to drug me and lock me away in a room in his house.

I wasn't about to sit around and wait to find out what he was going to do. I stood carefully and made my way slowly across the room. It wasn't a large room from what I could tell; there was a smooth wall against my palms after only twelve steps. I wasn't sure where I was in relation to the door, but if I kept my hands on the wall and moved around the room, I was bound to come to it eventually. I inched my way around the room, bumping into first one corner then another. I nearly took out my knees when I ran into the sofa, the only piece of furniture in the room. I stifled my instinct to cry out in surprise and continued my slow pace around the room. I went through all four corners of the room before I came to the door frame.

My fingers grasped the doorknob, and I turned it slowly, but it stopped halfway through the rotation. Locked. I dropped my head against the door in defeat and froze. I could hear Kendal talking to someone. I strained to make out the words.

"I know it's my problem. What was I supposed to do? She practically admitted that she saw us together." There was a pause, and I could only assume that the conversation was taking place over the phone. "No, she didn't accuse me of anything, but she did say that she remembered everything with 'crystal clarity' that happened before Chad grabbed her." Hold on. Kendal was on a first name basis with my attacker?

"That fucking idiot is on his own now." Another pause. "No, he's too loyal to snitch on us. I just need to make sure the bitch gets silenced and can't testify at the trial." Now I was a bitch? What type of life was Kendal leading that he associated with people who robbed drug stores and took lives without a second thought.

"I have a plan. She's been hanging around with this biker loser. I'm sure he has a rap sheet a mile long; it won't take much to convince the police that he had something to do with her disappearance. I'll let you know when it's done."

I stepped away from the door when I heard footsteps approach the door. My hands shook as I waited to see what Kendal would do. I wasn't where Kendal had left me and I hadn't encountered any light switches during my trip around the room. I had the element of surprise on my side, but the door didn't open. His footsteps continued down the hall. Fuck! I wanted to scream the word at the top of my lungs.

I pushed my hair back from my face and noticed that my hands were shaking. Why wouldn't they be shaking? I had just listened to someone I used to love and trust talk about how he was going to kill me, like it was just some chore he needed to take care of. Deep breaths, Autumn. You still have the element of surprise on your side. When he opens that door, you can turn the tables on him.

I took another step back from the door, leaned against the wall, and waited. I had nothing but time. Kendal probably thought that I was still unconscious but he had to know that it would wear off soon, and as much as he had changed since we had been together, I highly doubted that he would want to kill me when I was looking him in the eye. We had gone hunting once with his father, and he hadn't even been able to kill a squirrel because it was looking at him. My life had to mean more than a squirrel's, right?

I heard him making his way back to my door, and I tensed in anticipation. His footsteps stopped in front of the door, and I could hear Kendal mutter to himself, but it was too low for me to make out what he was saying.

Before I was ready, the door swung open, and I had to blink at the sudden intrusion of light that entered the room from the hallway. Kendal stepped into the doorway, the light at his back cast his face in shadows. A cold shiver of fear ran through my body at the ominous figure he presented.

"It's time, Auty. I can't put this off any longer." His voice was tender, which caused another cold shiver to roll down my back. He stepped into the room and approached the sofa. "Where are you?" He called out when he realized I wasn't where he had left me. I stayed silent and debated if I should make a run for it now or wait until he started looking for me.

"You can't hide from me for long. It's not that big of a room." He taunted.

But instead of looking for me like I expected him to, Kendal turned and made his way back toward the door and in doing so spotted me. I could tell the exact moment he did because an odd smile appeared on his face. "There you are."

Everything in me screamed at me to run now, but I stood my ground. Kendal was in better shape than I was, which meant that I wouldn't be able to escape if I didn't incapacitate him first. It wasn't until he was within touching distance that I noticed the knife in his hand. I had expected a gun, a knife, was more suited to a crime of passion. Of course, his plan was to frame Rusty. It made more sense now.

"I don't understand why you're doing this." I stalled for time, unsure how to proceed.

"Don't play dumb with me, Autumn. I saw the look you gave me last night when you admitted that you remembered everything from before you were taken hostage. I still can't believe that Chad picked you of all people to be his hostage. You saw us talking together before I went into the store."

"But I didn't." The denial fell from my lips before I could stop it. "I was too wrapped up in my own thoughts; that's how your friend snuck up on me."

"Even if that's true, you know too much now." Kendal said as he lunged at me without warning.

I raised my arm just in time to take a knife slash to the forearm instead of the chest. I cried out in pain and rage and lashed out with my foot, kicking Kendal in the shin. He slashed out with the knife again, and somehow I managed to dip out-of-the-way. I tried to shove him away from me, and he just laughed. He grabbed my left arm, the one that wasn't a bloody mess, and tugged me to him.

"This ends now." He pressed the knife to my neck, and I shuddered at the coldness of it. The pressure on my neck increased, and I could feel wetness start to pool in the indent of my collarbone.

I suddenly remembered the defense class I took my freshman year of college. Back then, I had laughed at the thought of anyone ever making unwanted advances on the fat girl, but now I was glad that it had been a mandatory seminar. I tensed my fingers and jabbed them straight into his eyes at the same time I stomped on his instep. The knife slipped down my throat, and he let go of my arm as he cried out in pain.

I put my hands on his shoulders and went for the final move. I jammed my knee straight into his crotch. He dropped the knife and doubled over, cupping his junk. I aimed one more kick at his injured groin to add insult to injury and then ran for the door.

"Stop." He choked out, like I would listen.

I slammed the door shut behind me and threw the lock. I saw my purse on the floor and scooped it up before heading for the front door. Sunlight had never looked so good. As I ran out the door, I could hear Kendal screaming behind me.

"I will fucking kill you! Get back here, Autumn!"

I continued to run, straight into a solid, warm body.

Chapter 13

MY BAD LUCK JUST KEPT getting worse. I'd escaped from one lunatic to run straight into the arms of... Rusty? With a black eye? What was he doing here?

"I installed a tracking app on your phone." I hadn't realized I had spoken out loud.

"You what?" I practically screeched.

"I only activated it when you didn't show up for work today but your car was in the parking lot. You can be mad at me later. Right now, we need to get those cuts looked at." At Rusty's words, I realized that the sun was closer to setting than it was to rising. Just how long had I been unconscious?

"What happened to your eye?" I asked as he wrapped an arm around my waist. It was only then that I noticed that on top of his usual t-shirt and jeans, Rusty was wearing a bulletproof vest and had a gun strapped to his hip. What in the world had happened while I was locked away in Kendal's house?

"Don't worry about it." He gave a sharp whistle, and I heard the fast approach of footsteps as we turned. The road behind us was lined with cop cars and two ambulances. Two paramedics rushed to my side as I stared around in confusion. "Victim has at least two visible wounds, one to the right forearm and one to the neck."

In an instant, Rusty morphed from the laid back biker I had grown to care for into a no-nonsense officer of the law, with a take charge attitude. "Suspect is still unaccounted for and should be considered armed and dangerous." He addressed the other officers as they approached us. They were dressed from head to toe in black and carried weapons I had only seen in movies and TV shows.

"I locked him in a room on the left side of the hallway." I called as the paramedics led me to one of the waiting ambulances for the second Friday in a row. This was a habit I needed to break pronto.

Kendal's screams of fury reached my ears as the police busted down his front door, and I briefly worried about Rusty's safety until the male paramedic started to disinfect the wound on my neck. "Ouch! A little warning would have been nice." I grumbled.

He grinned at me and continued his work. "You're lucky. This one isn't very deep at all. A couple of butterfly bandages and you'll be as good as new. Now that arm, on the other hand." He shook his head. "That one's going to need stitches, which means we're going to have to take you in." I cringed as he wrapped gauze lightly around my forearm.

The back door to the ambulance was still open, and I had the perfect view of Rusty as he led Kendal to the back of one of the waiting police cruisers. Kendal's right eye was swollen completely shut, and the left one didn't look much better. There were blood stains on his clothes, which I was almost positive were from me.

Rusty climbed into the back of the ambulance and slammed the doors shut behind him. "Let's go."

He had removed the bulletproof vest and once again looked every inch of a badass biker, complete with split knuckles that had already started to scab over, so Kendal's injuries must have been caused by me. Go me! I cheered to myself weakly.

"When were you going to tell me?" I asked.

"I wasn't."

"Great way to start a relationship, or was I just a cover?" I stared into his eyes and waited for his answer. The ache that started in my heart when he remained silent hurt far worse than any of my physical injuries.

Chapter 14

THIS TIME, I WAS RELEASED from the hospital after I received my stitches, all twenty-seven of them, and didn't have to sign myself out. Rusty called my mother to drive me home, and disappeared when she arrived. I wasn't sure if or when I would hear from again. I wasn't sure which betrayal hurt more, Kendal's or Rusty's. One tried to take my life, and the other stomped all over my heart.

"Do you want me to stay?" My mother asked when we pulled into my driveway.

"No. I think I need to be alone for a while." I didn't want an audience for my imminent breakdown.

"I love you. Call me in the morning." She patted my thigh, one of the few uninjured parts of my body.

"I will."

I had refused the prescription for painkillers that the doctor had offered and was starting to regret that decision. I swallowed a handful of ibuprofen and hoped that it would take the edge off the pain. Tomorrow, I would go about putting my life back in order, but tonight, I would wallow in my grief and heartache with whatever ice cream remained in my freezer.

I had just polished off a pint of mint chocolate chip when there was a knock on my front door. I considered ignoring it, but I wasn't sure who it could be. My normal visitors were out of commission, Kendal was behind bars and Rusty had ended our relationship with his silence. So much for a real relationship. A tear managed to escape, and I sniffled in an attempt to hold back the rest that were threatening to break free. Whoever was at the door knocked again, and I set my empty container on the kitchen counter before going to see who it was.

I opened the door to Rusty and nearly slammed it in his face, but I saw that he had brought my car home, so I stepped back and waited for him to come inside. I might as well get this over with now; just rip the band-aid off in one fell swoop.

"Can we talk?"

"If you want." I really wasn't in the mood to play nice.

"Stop acting like a victim."

"Isn't that what I am? I've been held hostage, shot, beat, kidnapped, drugged, and then attacked with a knife by someone I used to love. I think I deserve a few moments of self-pity, don't you?" I snarled at him, suddenly itching for a fight.

"No, I don't. You're stronger than that, Autumn. We both know that if anything, you're more pissed at me, so own that. Don't become some simpering, poor me girly girl. That's not who you are."

"You're right, I am pissed at you. You lied to me, and you couldn't even admit that you did." I crossed my arms across my chest and stared him down.

"Did you ever stop to think why?" He mimicked my stance. "You're a coward."

He laughed before responding. "You know that's not true. We had an audience. I'm not about to put my personal business out there for everyone. I respect you too much to let everyone be privy to the inner workings of our relationship."

"If you respected me, you wouldn't have lied to me for the last five months."

"I couldn't tell you. I've been undercover for the last three years, and only two people knew that fact. I finished the case I was working on last night, hence the black eye you asked about earlier. Now that the leader of the rival gang is no longer in charge, my stint as a biker is over. I can go back to being a normal street cop. The question is, do I stay here in Ivory or do I go back to Philly."

"Why would you stay here?"

"Why do you think?" He asked with a taunting grin.

"You miss your childhood home?"

"Are you always going to be this difficult? It's you; it's always been you. Why else would I jump at the chance to come back to this fishbowl of a town? I've been waiting for you since I was fifteen. Did you really think I didn't know who you were when I picked you up in the bar that night? I've been following you on social media for years. I knew that you were single, and I took my chance. It worked better than I could have ever hoped."

"My only regret was that I couldn't tell you what I really did for a living. I wanted to spend more time with you, but I had to do my job. I knew that I loved you after the first month of being together, but I couldn't tell you. I couldn't let anyone know that you meant anything to me. You had to be just someone I was screwing, at least to everyone looking at us from the outside. I tried to keep my distance in case things went south and I didn't survive this last week."

"Last Friday night, I knew that by this Friday things would be over one way or another, and I wanted others to see us together, even if it was just for a few minutes. You don't know how sorry I am that you got injured because of my selfishness."

"Wait... hold on just one second. Say that part again."

"Which part?"

"You know which part." I was in shock and tears threatened again, this time in happiness.

"I love you." I smiled at his soft proclamation.

"If this is going to work, we're going to need to have a talk about telling the truth."

"I agree completely. Whenever you want." Rusty took a step closer to me. When I didn't back away, he drew me into his arms. "Have anything you want to tell me? Since we're telling the truth now."

"Well..." I laughed at the feigned pained expression on his face. "I love you, too."

Stay in the Know

Visit Liza's Site: www.sweetanguish.com

Follow Liza on Instagram: @swtanguish

Join Liza on Facebook: Liza Kline - Author

Also by Liza Kline

A Joyous Romance

Betrothed to the Vampire King

Married to the Vampire King

Mated to the Vampire King

A Joyous Romance Series Bundle (Books 1-3)

Standalone

Cuffed - A Novella

The Trouble with Wedding Dates

The Fall of Diablo

Fated

The Princess & the Monk

About the Author

Liza Kline lives in eastern Pennsylvania where she devours romance novels and chocolate while waiting for the zombie apocalypse. Until that day comes, Liza enjoys trips to the beach, designing websites, taking too many photos of sunsets and going to rock concerts.

Made in the USA
Columbia, SC
02 November 2024

6a050129-d437-4015-92ff-4d8ea75856b2R01